Surf's Up!

Read more

MOBY SHINOBI AND TOBY TOO! books!

Take a Hike!

MOBY SHINOBI AND TOBY TOO!

SCHOLASTIC

Luke Flowers

Ready! Set! GO!

MOBY SHINOBI AND TOBY TOO!

SCHOLASTIC

Luke Flowers

BUILDING

忍
常
助
そ

Surf's Up!

Luke
Flowers

ACORN™
SCHOLASTIC INC.

For my brothers—Josh and Nathan. Thanks for all the memorable mayhem on the beaches of California, in the mountains of Colorado, and on the basketball courts of our childhood. It's a wonder we all survived those wild days! I love that I know you both as best friends, teammates, and heroes for life.

Library of Congress Cataloging-in-Publication Data

Names: Flowers, Luke, author, illustrator.
Title: Surf's up! / by Luke Flowers.
Description: First edition. | New York, NY : Scholastic Inc., 2020. | Series: Moby Shinobi and Toby too! | Summary: In rhyming text, Moby Shinobi and his dog Toby head to the beach for a day of fun, where Moby tries to put his ninja skill to work helping his friends build a sandcastle which unfortunately cannot withstand the weight of even a small ninja—however when a sailboat springs a leak, it is Moby Shinobi to the rescue.
Identifiers: LCCN 2018058517| ISBN 9781338547528 (pbk.) | ISBN 9781338547535 (reinforced library binding)
Subjects: LCSH: Ninja—Juvenile fiction. | Helping behavior—Juvenile fiction. | Sailboats—Juvenile fiction. | Seashore—Juvenile fiction. | Stories in rhyme. | CYAC: Stories in rhyme. | Ninja—Fiction. | Dogs—Fiction. | Helpfulness—Fiction. | Seashore—Fiction. | LCGFT: Stories in rhyme.
Classification: LCC PZ8.3.F672 Su 2020 | DDC [E]—dc23 LC record available at https://lccn.loc.gov/2018058517

10 9 8 7 6 5 4 3 2 1   20 21 22 23 24

Printed in China   62
First edition, January 2020
Edited by Samantha Swank and Rachel Matson
Book design by Sarah Dvojack

Table of Contents

WELCOME TO SHINOBI DOJO

HIYAH-5 NINJA ARTS

FARM PIZZA PETS FIREHOUSE BUILDING

TOBY

On the Go

Hi-yah! Hello, from our dojo!
Hey, ninja friend, where should we go?

Toby wants to play in the sun.
A trip to the beach would be fun!

3

Sunscreen, towels, and a beach ball.
Water and snacks. But that's not all!

Bo staff, nunchucks, rope, and a hook.
One last thing: a favorite book!

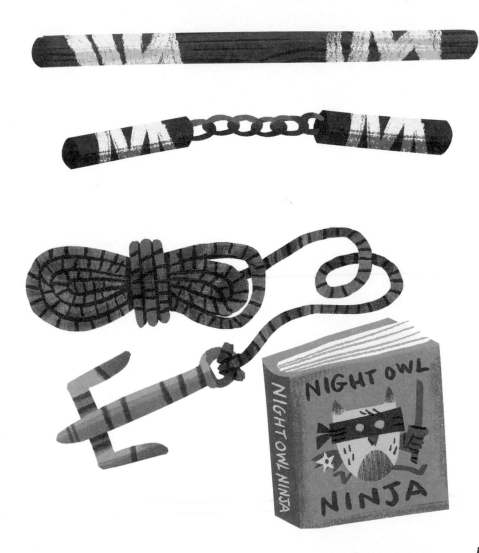

Moby rides with Toby in tow.
They howl and cheer—**Shinobi Go!**

It is the best part of the day.
We ninja-train while on our way!

Friends clap for super skateboard tricks!
Go! Double ninja twisting kicks!

Hot dog! Toby does a cool jump!

Whoa! Moby hops from stump to stump!

The beach is packed when they arrive.
They greet their friends with a high five!

Sun and Sand

The beach is full of ways to play.
This will be a great Beach Bash day!

Sandcastle building looks like fun!
Quick! The contest is almost done.

Moby thinks of a ninja flip.

He will plant the flag in a zip!

17

Moby's friends are covered in dust!
Their dreams of winning just went bust!

21

Wow! The crowd shouts when the dust clears.
Two proud ninjas soak in the cheers.

23

Catch of the Day

People fish and music plays.
The docks are great on sunny days.

Moby thinks of a quick rope throw.

He will hold on and not let go!

33

Let's swing and give the net a swish!
Together we will grab that fish!

The happy fishermen cheer, yoo-hoo!
This catch is a dream come true!

To the Rescue

SURF CONTEST

Boats sail along and flags fly free.
But what does Lifeguard Lucy see?

Look! Do you see the Captain's boat?
It sprang a leak and will not float!

41

With these tools, I know what to do!
Combine them all—make something new!

BO STAFF

ROPE

SHELLS

TOWEL

STICK

SURFBOARD

45

Hooray! The Captain grabs the line.
He and Polly will be just fine.

But then the blue sky turns pitch-black!
Can Moby tow his new crew back?

The wave crashes around the crew!

But Moby pulls them right on through.

They all land safely on the beach.
Polly lets out a happy **SCREECH**!

Big cheers go up from everywhere.
Moby is lifted up in the air!

Moby, you won the surf contest!
Your cool ninja moves were the best!

Ninjas play as the day goes by.
Then Lucy points up to the sky.

Toby yawns and lets out a sigh.
Now it is time to **wave** good-bye!

About the Author

Luke Flowers lives in Colorado Springs with his wife and three children. He LOVES going to the beach in California! He once stepped on a stingray and got a scary sting. However, like Moby,  he learned from his mistake and now charges into the surf like a brave ninja, careful of where he kicks.

Luke has illustrated over fifty books, including *New York Times* bestseller *A Beautiful Day in the Neighborhood* by Fred Rogers. But being able to write AND illustrate the Moby Shinobi series has been the most HIYAH-wesome highlight of his creative journey.

YOU CAN DRAW MOBY!

1 Draw a circle.

2 Draw a skinny oval. Add two more ovals and a half-circle to the side of the mask.

3 Add two ovals for the eyes. Fill in the pupils.

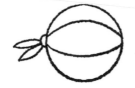

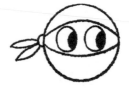

4 Finish the face. Draw the nose, mouth, and hair!

5 Draw a teardrop shape to make the body. Add arms, hands, legs, and feet!

6 Color in your drawing!

WHAT'S YOUR STORY?

Moby and Toby build a dragon sandcastle. Imagine that **you** are at the beach! What kind of sandcastle would you build? How would you use shells and kelp? Write and draw your story!

scholastic.com/acorn